Mr. Putter & Tabby Pick the Pears

CYNTHIA RYLANT

Mr. Putter & Tabby
Pick the Pears

Illustrated by

ARTHUR HOWARD

sandpiper

Houghton Mifflin Harcourt

Boston   New York

For Carolyn and Jim, who love the fall
— C. R.

For Rachel Mayeri
— A. H.

Text copyright © 1995 by Cynthia Rylant
Illustrations copyright © 2008, 1995 by Arthur Howard

www.hmhco.com

First Harcourt paperback edition 1995

Library of Congress Cataloging-in-Publication Data
Rylant, Cynthia.
Mr. Putter and Tabby pick the pears/Cynthia Rylant;
illustrated by Arthur Howard.—1st ed.
p.   cm.
Summary: When he gets too old to climb up the ladder,
Mr. Putter and his cat, Tabby, figure out an ingenious way
to pick pears for pear jelly.
[1. Fruit—Fiction.   2. Old age—Fiction.   3. Cats—Fiction.]
I. Howard, Arthur, ill.   II. Title.
PZ7.R982Ms   1995
[Fic]—dc20   94-11259
ISBN 978-0-15-200245-9 hc
ISBN 978-0-15-200246-6 pb

Manufactured in China

SCP   30 29
4500525091

1

Pear Jelly

It was fall,

and juicy things were growing

in Mr. Putter's backyard.

Juicy apples, juicy tomatoes,

juicy pears.

Mr. Putter walked with
his fine cat, Tabby,
among the juicy things,
and he dreamed.
He dreamed of apple pie
and apple turnovers.
He dreamed of hot apple cider
with a cinnamon stick,
and stuffed red tomatoes.

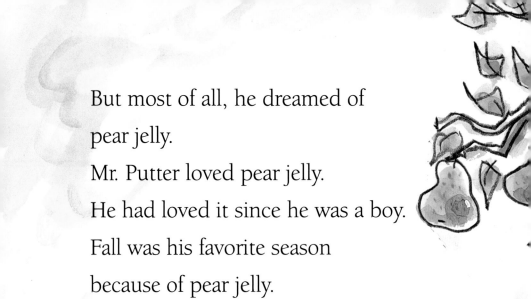

But most of all, he dreamed of
pear jelly.
Mr. Putter loved pear jelly.
He had loved it since he was a boy.
Fall was his favorite season
because of pear jelly.

And now it was time.

"Tabby," said Mr. Putter, "it is time to pick the pears."

Tabby loved it when Mr. Putter
said it was time to do something.
She was old, but she still
liked excitement.
She followed Mr. Putter
into the garage,
where he found a ladder
for pear picking.

Then they went to the backyard—
where all the excitement was.

2
Cranky Legs

Mr. Putter had a problem.

It was a ladder problem.

Mr. Putter set his ladder

against the pear tree.

But he couldn't get up the ladder.

Last year he got up the ladder.

But this year he had cranky legs.

Cranky legs, cranky knees,

cranky feet.

He stepped onto the ladder,
and his legs were so cranky
he had to get right off again.
"One trouble with being old,"
said Mr. Putter, "is being cranky."
Tabby knew what he meant.

She had a cranky tail.
Some days it was so cranky
it wouldn't swish.
It just stuck in the air
like a stick.
Cranky legs and cranky tails
are no fun when you're old.
Especially if you want pear jelly.

Mr. Putter looked at
the pears still in his tree,
and he thought.
He thought and thought
and thought.
Tabby curled herself up
and waited.
She liked excitement.
But she could wait for it.

3

ZING!!!!!

"What I need," said Mr. Putter at last,
"is a good slingshot."
Mr. Putter knew about slingshots.
He had played with them as a boy.
They were good for knocking
cans off logs.
So they must be good for knocking
pears off trees.
Tabby followed him into the house
to make a slingshot.

Mr. Putter found a pair of
old underwear that he didn't like.
He didn't like it because
it was covered with poodles.
His brother had given him the
underwear for his birthday.
His brother loved the underwear.
He thought it was funny.
Mr. Putter did not.

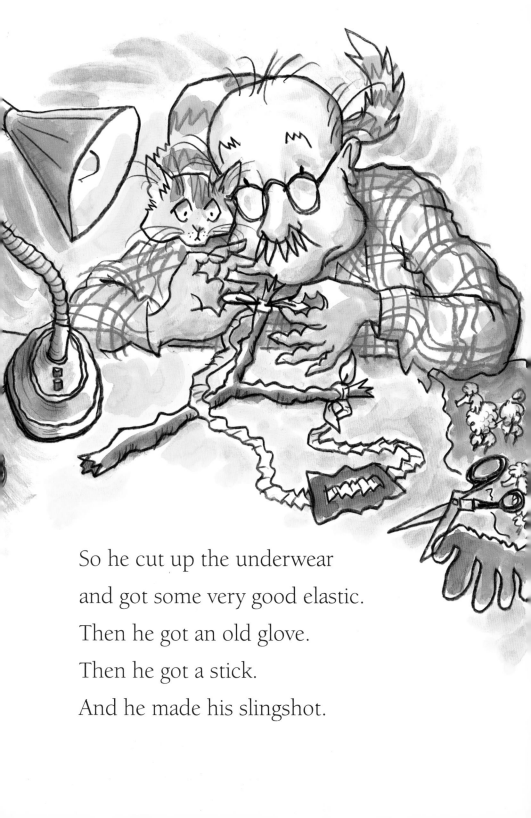

So he cut up the underwear
and got some very good elastic.
Then he got an old glove.
Then he got a stick.
And he made his slingshot.

Mr. Putter and Tabby went back
to the pear tree.
Mr. Putter needed something hard
and round to sling.

Many of his apples had already fallen.
So he picked up an apple.

He put the apple in the slingshot.
He aimed at a pear in the tree
and pulled back as hard as he could.

ZING!!!!!
The hard, round apple went flying
up, up, up.
Over Mr. Putter's pear tree.
Over Mr. Putter's apple tree.
Over Mr. Putter's chimney.
Over Mr. Putter's house.

Mr. Putter and Tabby watched
as it flew out of sight.
"*Hmmm,*" said Mr. Putter.
He picked up another apple.

ZING!!!!!

Up, up, up.

Over, over, over.

Out of sight.

"Wow!" said Mr. Putter.

He was smiling.

He might have cranky legs.
But he sure had jiffy hands.
He picked up another apple.

ZING!!!!!
Another apple.

ZING!!!!!

Another.

ZING!!!!!
He forgot all
about the pears.

Tabby liked the first zings.

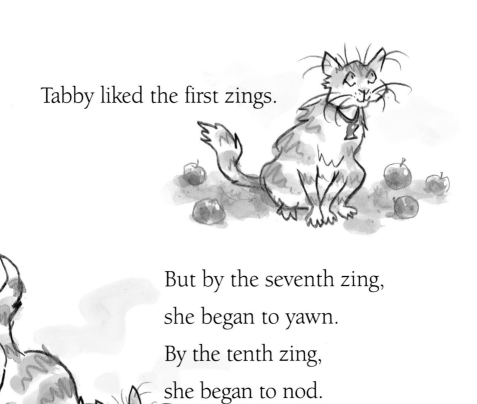

But by the seventh zing,

she began to yawn.

By the tenth zing,

she began to nod.

And by the fourteenth zing,

she was sound asleep.

Mr. Putter played with his slingshot
all afternoon.
He played through teatime.

He played through suppertime.

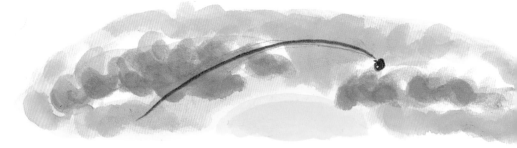

He played until dark,
when he couldn't see the apples
go up anymore.

When he was finished,
he had no apples
and no pear jelly.
He was a little embarrassed.
He picked up Tabby
and sneaked inside.

4

Juicy Days

The next afternoon,
Mr. Putter and Tabby
were sitting on their porch.
They were feeling sorry for themselves
because they still had no pear jelly.

Suddenly Mr. Putter's neighbor
Mrs. Teaberry and her good dog,
Zeke, came by.
Mrs. Teaberry was carrying
a big basket,
a *very* big basket.
She said to Mr. Putter,
"It is amazing.
When I woke up this morning,
there were dozens of apples
in my front yard.
And I don't even
have an apple tree!"

Mr. Putter looked at Tabby.

"Amazing!" he said.

"So I made an apple feast!"

said Mrs. Teaberry.

In the basket she had
fourteen apple turnovers,
five apple pies,
six apple jellies,
and a gallon of hot apple cider
with cinnamon sticks.

Mr. Putter and Tabby ate juicy things
for days and days.
And when he was finishing the
last apple pie,
Mr. Putter had an idea about those pears
still on his pear tree.

He would wait for them all
to fall off . . .

. . . then he would get his slingshot.

And start zinging!

The illustrations in this book were done in pencil, watercolor,
gouache, and Sennelier pastels on 90-pound vellum paper.
The display type was set in Minya Nouvelle, Agenda, and Artcraft.
The text type was set in Berkeley Old Style Book.
Color separations by Bright Arts, Ltd., Singapore
Printed and bound by RR Donnelley, China
Production supervision by Warren Wallerstein and Kent MacElwee
Series cover design by Kristine Brogno and Michele Wetherbee
Cover design by Brad Barrett
Designed by Arthur Howard and Carolyn Stafford-Griffin